ATTACK ON
DELRAKKIN

#3

ATTACK ON DELRAKKIN

RYDER WINDHAM

SCHOLASTIC INC.

New York Toronto London Auckland Sydney

ISBN 0-590-12795-0

12 11 10 9 8 7 6 5 4   8 9/9 0 1 2/0

Printed in the U.S.A.

First Scholastic printing, November 1997

ATTACK ON DELRAKKIN

INTRODUCTION

After the Death Star was destroyed, Luke Skywalker and the Rebel Alliance discovered the Imperial space station had carried a cargo of bacta, a chemical compound used to treat and heal wounds. Later, the Rebels learned the Death Star's bacta was contaminated. Princess Leia Organa believed they had uncovered a secret Imperial plan to poison an entire world and feared the plan might not have ended with the destruction of the Death Star.

Looking for clues, the Rebels left their base on Yavin Four and traveled to Thyferra, the only planet in the galaxy capable of producing bacta. On Thyferra, the Rebels were told of an Imperial shipment of alazhi, a plant used in bacta production. The alazhi was sent to Delrakkin, a planet at the end of an old hyperspace trade route.

Now, the Rebels prepared to leave for the Outer Rim . . . unaware of the danger awaiting them on Delrakkin.

PRELIMINARY MISSION

CHAPTER ONE

The Death Star was gone. Grand Moff Tarkin and 265,000 Imperial soldiers were dead.

If the news had not come from Emperor Palpatine, Admiral Termo would not have believed it.

Termo stood in his private quarters aboard the Imperial Star Destroyer *Liquidator* and gazed out beyond the viewport. He tried to focus on the planet Delrakkin, but his mind was in turmoil. He could not stop thinking about the hologrammic conversation he'd just had with the Emperor. *The Emperor himself!*

There was no record of the conversation, but Termo remembered every word.

"What happened to the Death Star?" Termo had asked the Emperor's hologram.

The Emperor had responded with a sinister laugh. "That is not your concern! What were your last orders from Tarkin?"

"We were to wait at Delrakkin for further instructions," Termo had replied. "In the event the Death Star did not reach the Delrakkin system, Tarkin entrusted me with three holotapes. The first holotape carried instructions to contact you."

"I *know* that, Admiral Termo," Palpatine had sneered. "Tell me what you know about alazhi."

Termo had cleared his throat. "Alazhi is the plant used in the production of bacta. Until now, alazhi has only grown on the planet Thyferra."

"Your Captain Skeezer transported a shipment of alazhi from Thyferra a few weeks ago?"

"Yes, Emperor. The alazhi was brought to Delrakkin. A covert squadron planted the alazhi in an area west of Delrakkin City."

Emperor Palpatine nodded. "And do you know why Tarkin ordered you to plant the alazhi on Delrakkin?"

"I assumed to see if it would grow. Except for the storms, Delrakkin's atmosphere and climates are similar to those on Thyferra. Am I correct in my assumption?"

Palpatine had shaken his head. "You really *don't* know anything, do you, Admiral?"

Admiral Termo had grimaced. "Perhaps, Emperor, if you were to tell me about the Death Star, I might know —" Suddenly, Termo's words had caught in his throat. He couldn't breathe. The Emperor had reached out with the Force to choke him.

Palpatine's hologram had smiled sinisterly as Termo struggled. "If you tell anyone of the Death Star's destruction, you will die by the power of the dark side of the Force!"

Palpatine then had released his supernatural grip. "Emperor!" Termo had gasped. "I . . . I beg you to forgive me for speaking out of turn. I await your orders."

"You'll find your orders on the second holotape!" Palpatine had snapped, his hologram flickering slightly. "There has been one change in the plans. The Death Star was carrying a large shipment of bacta. The bacta was to be delivered to the survivors of the attack on Delrakkin City. This is no longer a possibility."

"Delrakkin City?" Termo had asked. "I'm afraid I don't

understand, Emperor. There hasn't been any attack on Delrakkin City."

A grotesque smile had played across Palpatine's withered face. "Ahh," sighed Palpatine. "But there *will* be!" The hologram had flickered again and then had vanished into the air.

None of it made any sense, Termo now thought. *What could alazhi be used for besides bacta production? What was the purpose of this mission? Could it be more important than the destruction of the Death Star?* It seemed impossible.

Termo's pulse was slowly returning to normal. He held his hand to his throat. There didn't appear to be any damage.

Termo inserted the second holotape into the projector. The image of Grand Moff Tarkin appeared. Termo blinked, aware that he was looking at a dead man.

"Admiral Termo," Tarkin's hologram began. "I hope your conversation with the Emperor went well, but imagine it did not. I'm making this recording to insure that you will carry out your mission on Delrakkin."

Tarkin's hologram continued to speak for five minutes. When the holotape ended, Termo tapped into the ship's comm. "Admiral Termo to the bridge," he stated. "Leave Delrakkin's orbit immediately and take us to the far side of the nearest moon."

After Han Solo secured the Y-wing starfighter to the lower hull of the *Millennium Falcon*, the *Falcon* blasted away from the Thyferran spaceport. Chewbacca rapidly keyed the nav computer for the route to the Delrakkin system. Solo threw the thrust initiator and the *Falcon* leaped into the explosive flow of hyperspace.

In the cockpit of the *Falcon*, Princess Leia Organa and Luke Skywalker were belted into the seats behind Solo and Chewbacca. See-Threepio, Artoo-Detoo, and the ancient droid Q-7N were in the central hold area.

"Do you know anything about the Delrakkin system?" Leia asked Solo.

"A little," Solo answered. "It's not far from the end of an old hyperspace trade route to the Outer Rim. Besides Delrakkin, there are two other planets in the system, but neither of them supports any life."

"What about Delrakkin itself?" Luke asked.

"It's a jungle planet with a native population. There's a lot of storm activity on the surface. Spacers say Delrakkin's greatest natural resource is its bad weather. It's so nasty that most natives live underground. Delrakkin City was the only civilized place on the planet. It was built high on a mountain, above the clouds and the lousy weather."

"You've been to Delrakkin?"

"No," Solo replied. "But word got around that Delrakkin City used to be a good place for smugglers to hide out."

"Why isn't it a good place to hide anymore?" Luke inquired.

Chewbacca didn't turn to Luke but allowed a low snarl to rumble from his muzzle.

After an awkward silence, Luke asked, "Did I say something wrong?"

"The native Delrakkins were said to be very hospitable to travelers," Solo replied, "but that was before they were forced out of their own city by the Empire."

At the mention of the Empire, Chewbacca roared. Leia and Luke cringed in their seats.

Solo shook his head as he pretended to reprimand his copilot. "How many times do I have to tell you, Chewie?" Solo asked. "If you scare the passengers, they won't fly with us anymore!"

"What happened to the native Delrakkins?" Leia wanted to know.

"The Empire let them stay," Solo replied. "The only catch is the natives aren't allowed into Delrakkin City. The city is only for Imperial citizens."

"Why was the Empire so interested in Delrakkin?"

"Beats me. Maybe they've got a research center or something, but I don't know what they'd be studying out there. Like I said, Delrakkin is mostly one big rainstorm."

Leia gazed out the cockpit at the dazzling light cascading through hyperspace. "It doesn't make sense," she uttered. "The Carrack cruiser transported alazhi to Delrakkin — but why? We know the Death Star was carrying contaminated bacta — perhaps to the same destination. Was the Empire planning on growing bacta to heal or to use as a weapon?"

"We don't *know* that the Death Star had anything to do with Delrakkin," Solo countered. "All we know is the Carrack cruiser that recently crashed on Yavin Four is the same ship that transported alazhi from Thyferra to Delrakkin."

"Don't forget it was the Carrack's captain who told us the Death Star's cargo was contaminated!" Leia responded. "Han, the bacta is the *connection*. Someone in the Delrakkin system must have been waiting for the Death Star.

When the Death Star didn't arrive, the Carrack was sent to the Yavin system to investigate."

Han shrugged. "It's possible," he admitted. "But if someone sent the Carrack cruiser, that someone might still be waiting at Delrakkin."

"The Carrack could have been carried by an Imperial Star Destroyer," suggested Luke.

"Then we should take a little precaution," Solo said as he rapidly adjusted several switches on the nav computer.

"What did you just do?" asked Leia.

The captain of the *Millennium Falcon* grinned. "You'll see when we get there!"

CHAPTER TWO

Admiral Termo surveyed the twenty-four Imperial pilots in the bay of the *Liquidator.* Lieutenant Kevell, a lean young officer, stood at attention before the pilots. Kevell had assumed the position of the missing Captain Skeezer.

"We have positioned the *Liquidator* on the far side of Delrakkin's closest moon," began Termo, "to prepare for an attack. However, we do not want our opponent to know the attack came from the *Liquidator.*"

Termo gazed at Kevell and continued. "Imperial spies have discovered that the citizens of Delrakkin have joined the Rebel Alliance. Even worse, the citizens believe they can grow bacta on Delrakkin. Obviously, we do not want the Rebels to have their own supply of bacta."

Termo stepped forward and faced a single black-armored pilot. The admiral could see his own reflection in the black lenses of the pilot's helmet as he said, "Delrakkin has betrayed the Empire."

Termo turned and paced slowly before the pilots. "It is the will of Emperor Palpatine that the Delrakkin citizens be crushed." Termo paused. "However, the galaxy must believe that Delrakkin was crushed *not* by the Empire, but by the Rebel Alliance!"

The admiral came to a stop beside Kevell. "When word spreads that the Rebels attacked Delrakkin in order to take over the bacta production," stated Termo, "no planet in the galaxy will trust the Alliance!"

* * *

The *Millennium Falcon* blew out of hyperspace, and the view from the cockpit quickly shifted into realspace. There were no planets in sight.

"Where are we?" Leia asked. "Are you sure this is the Delrakkin system?"

"What were you expecting?" Solo scoffed. "Maybe a giant sign that says THIS WAY TO DELRAKKIN? Think again, Your Lostlessness." Solo flipped a series of switches. "We left hyperspace short of our destination so we could make our approach at sublight. If there are any Imperials waiting, I want to see them before they see us." The *Falcon* launched toward the Delrakkin system.

"It's good to know you're thinking ahead, for a change," Leia murmured.

"Excuse me," Luke said as he unbuckled himself from his seat. "I'm going to check on the droids."

Luke walked to the central hold area. Artoo and Q-7N were engaged in a complicated match at the gaming table. Threepio looked up from his seat. "Hello, Master Luke. Are we nearing Delrakkin?"

"We're getting there," replied Luke as he kicked at the floor.

The golden droid tilted his head to one side and said, "May I ask if there's anything wrong?"

"Oh, it's nothing," Luke replied. "Leia and Han were just bickering again."

"Ah, the bickering," Threepio sighed. "They do it so often, I sometimes think they actually enjoy it!"

"That's what I'm afraid of," Luke mumbled.

CHAPTER THREE

In the *Liquidator*'s secondary launch bay, Lieutenant Kevell led the Imperial pilots past two TIE fighters. Kevell approached a wide black metal door that led to another hangar. He raised one hand and the pilots halted.

"Squadron One will attack the north end of Delrakkin City," Kevell instructed, "and Squadron Two will take the south. My wingman and I will follow you in our TIE fighters to verify your progress."

Kevell entered a code into a wall panel, and the wide hangar door slid slowly down into the floor. "Any survivors of Delrakkin City must believe this attack came from the Rebel Alliance," stated Kevell. "Fortunately, we were ready for such a mission."

The twenty-four Imperial pilots turned to look at their ships. Inside the hangar were twenty-four X-wing starfighters.

"Prepare for immediate takeoff," ordered Kevell.

"There's Delrakkin," Solo said as the *Millennium Falcon* zoomed toward the green planet. "Our sensors aren't picking up any Imperial signals."

"Wait!" Leia cried, pointing to a small cluster of moving lights. "Look over there! Are those satellites or ships?"

Chewbacca growled.

"They're ships," Solo answered as he drew closer. "They almost look like —"

"X-wings!" Leia interrupted. "There must be twenty of them!"

"Two dozen," Han corrected. "But who's piloting them? There aren't any Rebel outposts this far out."

The twenty-four X-wings veered off their course and angled toward the *Falcon*.

"It appears we've been spotted," observed Leia. "They're heading our way. We'd better hope they're friendly."

Chewbacca snarled.

"Forget friendly, Princess!" Solo yelled. "Those may be X-wings, but they're flying in a TIE-fighter attack formation! Chewie, go to full shields and evasive maneuvers while I charge the main guns!" Solo sprang from his seat and ran to the central hold area. "Luke! We've got trouble!"

The *Falcon* shuddered under a sudden barrage of laser fire.

"What is it?" Luke asked, sprinting after Solo.

"We're under attack by X-wings!" Solo answered as he climbed to the topside gunport.

"X-wings?!" Luke nearly slipped as he rushed down to the lower gunport.

"They're piloted by Imperials!" Solo called into his headset as he adjusted his laser cannon. "No time for questions. Just blast 'em!"

Luke gazed through the transparisteel windows as he belted himself into his seat. The only ship he saw was the Y-wing starfighter secured to the *Falcon*'s hull, but he sensed the oncoming danger.

Solo activated his targeting computer. Luke reached for his, then remembered his experience at the Death Star and the words of Obi-Wan Kenobi. *Remember*, Ben's voice had said, *the Force will be with you . . . always*. Luke took a deep breath and pushed the targeting computer aside.

Three X-wings fired at the *Falcon* as they flew into Solo's view. Solo swiveled in his gun mount, squeezing off a furious series of shots at the X-wings. Two laser blasts contacted with a fusial thrust engine on one X-wing. The starfighter exploded in a shower of screaming metal.

Five X-wings soared toward Luke's gunport. Luke reached out with the Force, sensing the starfighters' speeding positions as he hammered his guns. He opened his eyes to see two X-wings detonate against the stars.

The *Millennium Falcon* rocked hard as its shields were bombarded with more laser fire.

"Get us out of here, Chewbacca!" Leia ordered, still in the cockpit. "There's too many of them!"

The *Falcon* dove between six starfighters as Chewbacca struggled to avoid the oncoming laserblasts. One X-wing flew head-on toward the *Falcon*, and Chewbacca tried to avoid the ship, banking hard to the right. The X-wing wavered, then slammed and exploded against the *Falcon*'s hull. Instantly, a warning light blinked in the *Falcon*'s cockpit.

Chewbacca yelled to Solo over the comm.

"We've lost the deflector shield projector?!" Han said worriedly. "Head for the planet's surface!"

The *Falcon* plunged through Delrakkin's mesosphere, followed by the twenty remaining X-wing starfighters. The *Falcon*'s engines screeched through the sky as Chewbacca steered through rain clouds toward a prominent mountain range.

The lead X-wing fired, and the blasts impacted against two of the *Falcon*'s drive units. Smoke trailed from behind the freighter as it plummeted to the jungle below.

"Head for those rock formations at the edge of the jungle, Chewie!" Solo yelled into the comm. "I'm going to fire a concussion missile! Hit the inertial dampers on three!"

From years of working together, Chewbacca instantly knew Solo's plan. Solo counted to three and fired the missile as Chewbacca brought the *Falcon* to a violent, shuddering stop. The missile detonated against the mountainside, sending stone and clouds of dust into the air as Chewbacca rapidly reversed. Under the cover of rain and dust, Chewbacca skillfully landed the *Falcon* below the trees.

Leia ran from the cockpit to the gunport hatch.

"What did you just do?!" Luke screamed as he scrambled out of the hatch after Solo.

"I just saved our skins, kid," Solo replied calmly. "I fired the missile ahead of us while Chewie hit the brakes. To the Imperials behind us, it looked like we crashed!"

"It was a reckless maneuver," Leia observed, "but it worked. The X-wings took off!"

"Well, what are we going to do now?" Luke asked as he climbed out of the hatch.

"The *Falcon* needs repairs before she's going anywhere," Solo muttered.

"But the *Falcon* didn't take any hits below!" Luke exclaimed. "There's no damage to our Y-wing. One of us can go after those starfighters!"

"Are you serious?!" Solo asked.

"Luke's right," Leia admitted. "There's no telling what those Imperial pilots are plotting. One of us has to go after those X-wings and stop them!"

MISSION
BRIEFING

Before you proceed, you must consult the Mission Guide for the rules of the STAR WARS MISSIONS. You must follow these rules at all times.

This is a Rebel mission.

The *Millennium Falcon* has been damaged in a battle against two squadrons of X-wings piloted by Imperial soldiers. Four X-wings were destroyed, but the remaining twenty are still at large. After an emergency landing on the planet Delrakkin, you will pilot a Y-wing starfighter and pursue the Imperial pilots.

Your goal is to stop the Imperial pilots and find out the nature of their mission. To gain this information, you will need to find the Imperial pilots' base of operations. If the X-wing attack is part of the Empire's bacta conspiracy, you have even more reason to uncover the location of the base. Do not forget there are native creatures on the planet Delrakkin. The natives know more about their planet than anyone else, so you should try to work with them.

You start this mission with your Mission Point (MP) total from your previous Mission on Thyferra. (If this is your first Mission, you begin with 1000 MP).

Choose your character. You can take no more than four weapons (including a blaster rifle and a blaster pistol) and three vehicles (including a speeder bike). You can use your Powers twice in this Mission.

May the Force be with you.

Your Mission: Attack on Delrakkin

Rain beats down on the jungle of Delrakkin. The Y-wing starfighter has been separated from the *Millennium Falcon*. You raise the Y-wing's transparisteel canopy and climb into the seat. It occurs to you that you may be embarking on your most dangerous mission. Suddenly, Q-7N flies up next to you and hovers beside your head.

"Wish me luck, Q-7N," you say, forcing a grin. "It looks like I'm going to need it if I'm going to stop twenty X-wings."

"Actually, I've talked it over with the others," Q-7N replies, "and they agree I should go with you. I believe I could be of great assistance to you if —"

"Okay!" you interrupt the floating droid. "Get in back."

The droid drops into the backseat as you pull the canopy down. Heavy raindrops pelt the window.

Your friends are already at work on the *Falcon*'s deflector shield projector and drive units. They turn and look in your direction. Knowing that there's a chance they may never see you again, no one wants to wave good-bye. You smile and give them a thumbs-up signal as you lift the Y-wing off the jungle floor.

Q-7N gazes up to the sky as you fly low over the trees. "Why would Imperial pilots fly in X-wing starfighters?"

"My guess is they're on a covert mission," you answer. "The pilots are obviously pretending to be Rebels. The Empire is trying to trick someone."

"How do you know where to find the X-wings?" asks Q-7N.

"Believe it or not, I'm only guessing. But since Delrakkin City is the Imperial center on this planet, I figure it's the best place to start looking."

"What if the X-wings are somewhere else?" inquires Q-7N.

"You ask a lot of questions for a droid," you chuckle.

Q-7N seems to consider this for a moment. "How else am I going to learn anything?" Q-7N turns his gaze down to the jungle below. "You seem to be flying terribly close to the trees."

"I'm hoping to stay below the level of the Imperial sensors," you explain. "Unless some pilots locate us visually, we should be able to make it to Delrakkin City in just a few —"

Laser fire interrupts your conversation with Q-7N. The lethal bolts strike the trees in front of you.

"Stang!" you exclaim. "Someone's shooting at me from above!"

Q-7N aims a photoreceptor at an odd angle to gaze outside the canopy. "There are two small, spherical ships. Each has flat hexagonal wings," observes the droid.

"TIE fighters!" you exclaim as you straighten out your flight path.

"Identify yourself!" a voice hails over the Y-wing's comm. "You are flying within Imperial territory! I repeat, identify yourself!" You turn off the comm.

"Can you outrun them?" Q-7N whispers from behind.

"Not a chance. TIE fighters are faster than any Y-wing. But we're going to have to do something if we want to stay alive!" You pull back on the control shift, and the Y-wing arcs upward against the rain.

You can either evade or combat the TIE fighters. Choose now.

To evade the TIE fighters (without Power): Add your skill# to your Y-wing's stealth# +3 for your confront#. Roll the 12-dice to evade the TIE fighters.

If your confront# is equal to or more than your roll#, add the difference to your MP total and proceed.

If your confront# is lower than your roll#, subtract the difference from your MP total. You were not able to successfully dodge the TIE fighters and must now combat them. Choose now to combat both TIE fighters at once or one at a time, then proceed (below).

To evade the TIE fighters (using Power)*: Choose your Vehicle Evasion Power. Add your skill# and Jedi# to your Power's low-resist# and your vehicle's stealth# for your confront#. Roll the 6-dice to evade the two TIE fighters.

If your confront# is equal to or more than your roll#, add the difference to your MP total and proceed.

If your confront# is lower than your roll#, subtract the difference from your MP total. You were not able to successfully dodge the TIE fighters and must now combat them. Choose now to combat both TIE fighters at once or one at a time, then proceed (below).

*Note: This counts as one of two Power uses you are allowed in this Mission.

To combat both TIE fighters at once: Add your stealth# to your Y-wing's weaponry# +1 for your confront#. Roll the 12-dice to loop behind the TIE fighters and fire a shot that will blast one ship into the other's path, causing both ships to collide.

If your confront# is equal to or more than your roll#, add 8 MP to your MP total. The TIE fighters have collided and crashed. You may proceed.

If your confront# is lower than your roll#, subtract the difference from your MP total. Now double your confront# for your new confront#. Roll the 12-dice again to continue to fire at the TIE fighters.

If your new confront# is equal to or more than your roll#, add the difference to your MP total. The TIE fighters have crashed and you may proceed.

If your new confront# is less than your roll#, subtract the difference from your MP total. You must now proceed to combat the TIE fighters one at a time (below).

To combat the TIE fighters one at a time: Add your stealth# to your Y-wing's weaponry# for your confront#. Roll the 6-dice to combat the first TIE fighter. When you have defeated the first TIE fighter, you may proceed to combat the second one.

If your confront# is equal to or more than your roll#, add the difference to your MP total. You may proceed to combat the second TIE fighter, using the same confront equation.

If your confront# is less than your roll#, subtract the difference from your MP total and repeat this confront, adding +1 to your confront# for your new confront#. Once you have defeated the first TIE fighter, repeat this confront for the second TIE fighter using your first confront#. Once you have defeated the second TIE fighter, you may proceed.

After you have evaded or destroyed the two TIE fighters, add 20MP to your MP total (35 for Advanced Level players).

In the distance ahead, a massive mountain looms across the horizon. The top of the mountain is lost in heavy rain clouds.

"We don't want any Imperials to spot us above the cloudline," you relay to Q-7N, "so we're going to hug the side of the mountain all the way to the top."

You steer the Y-wing into a sharp, vertical climb. The mountainside races past the bottom of the ship at a horrifying speed.

Suddenly, the unmistakable sound of laser fire pierces the air, and the mountain explodes in front of you. A shower of small rocks hammers down on the Y-wing's transparisteel canopy.

"What was that?!" Q-7N shouts.

The dust clears and you see a turret built into the mountainside. "There's an ion cannon up ahead!" you exclaim.

The massive barrel of the ion cannon locks back as it prepares to fire again.

The ion cannon has locked its targeting computer onto

your ship. A burst of ion energy will severely damage your Y-wing's mechanical and computer systems. You must destroy the ion cannon.

To destroy the ion cannon: Add your weaponry# and your Y-wing's weaponry# to your skill# for your confront#. Roll the 12-dice to fire a proton torpedo at the ion cannon.

If your confront# is equal to or more than your roll#, add 7 MP to your MP total. The ion cannon explodes into Imperial rubble. You may now proceed.

If your confront# is lower than your roll#, subtract the difference from your MP total. Now add +3 to your confront# for your new confront#. Roll the 12-dice again to fire another proton torpedo at the devastating ion cannon.

If your new confront# is equal to or more than your roll#, add the difference to your MP total, then proceed.

If your new confront# is less than your roll#, subtract the difference from your MP total. Repeat this confront with your new confront# until you have destroyed the ion cannon. After the cannon is destroyed, you may proceed.

The ion cannon explosion tears at your Y-wing as you soar up the mountainside, but your shields hold. Seconds later, the Y-wing shoots above the rain clouds. You emerge at the top of the mountain and get your first view of Delrakkin City.

Towering skyscrapers are in flames. Crashed landspeeders lie overturned in the streets. The X-wings are swarming everywhere, firing lasers and torpedoes at buildings as Imperial citizens run for their lives.

"The Imperials are attacking their own city!" Q-7N cries.

The awesome truth immediately strikes you. "They're faking a Rebel attack!"

"What should we do?"

"Hang on to your cogitative theory unit," you advise as you adjust your laser cannons. "We're not going to let the Empire get away with this! We're going to show those Imperial pilots a *real* Rebel attack!"

Two X-wings come screeching into your firing range.

Choose now to combat both X-wings at once or one at a time, then proceed.

To combat both X-wings at once: Add your skill# and your weaponry# to your Y-wing's weaponry# +1 for your confront#. Roll the 12-dice to fire.

If your confront# is equal to or more than your roll#, add the difference to your MP total. The Imperial pilots try to dodge the blast, but both smash into a burning building. You may now proceed.

If your confront# is lower than your roll#, subtract the difference from your MP total. Repeat this confront until you have defeated the two X-wings, then proceed.

To combat one X-wing at a time: Your weaponry# + your vehicle's weaponry# is your confront#. Roll the 6-dice to fire your laser cannons at the first X-wing.

If your confront# is equal to or more than your roll#, add the difference to your MP total. You may proceed to the second X-wing, using the same confront equation.

If your confront# is less than your roll#, subtract the difference from your MP total and repeat this confront, adding +2 to your confront# for your new confront#. Once you have defeated the first X-wing, repeat this confront for the second X-wing using your first confront#. After you have defeated the second X-wing, you may proceed.

You have defeated two Imperial-piloted X-wings. Add 15MP to your MP total.

"Good shooting!" Q-7N praises.

"Thanks," you mutter as you scan the smoke-filled sky, "but there are still eighteen more ships left."

"Look out!" the droid yells. "On your starboard side!"

Three distant X-wings soar away from their bombing run on the city and race toward you.

"I see them," you reply as you swoop down to the city streets. An alley between two burning buildings appears to be the best route of escape. The Y-wing's engines howl as you punch the accelerator.

You enter the alley at breakneck speed, trusting your terrain-following sensors to keep you at a steady height above the ground. On either side of the Y-wing, Imperial office buildings are aflame. Above you, scaffolding, ventilation pipes, and walkways clutter the space between the buildings.

The three X-wings enter the alley behind you, firing deadly laser blasts at your ship. On the Y-wing's cockpit dashboard, a red warning light begins blinking madly.

"What's wrong now?" Q-7N asks.

"There's a dead end up ahead!" you answer. "Sensors indicate it's a stone barrier! And we can't go up — we'll have to go through it!"

"Through it?!" Q-7N cries.

To blast through the stone barrier: Your skill# + your Y-wing's weaponry# +3 is your confront#. Roll the 12-dice to fire a proton torpedo and blast a Y-wing-sized tunnel through the wall.

If your confront# is equal to or more than your roll#, add the difference to your MP total. You have blasted through the wall. Debris explodes around you as you fly forward.

If your confront# is less than your roll#, subtract the difference from your MP total. Add +1 to your confront# and repeat this confront with your new confront# until you have blasted through the wall. After you have shattered the wall, you can proceed.

The Y-wing flies through the demolished wall and emerges in another alleyway. Behind you, three explosions erupt as the barrier comes crashing down on top of the X-wings. The shock wave from the blast propels the Y-wing even faster through the air.

The alley opens up to a main street. Imperial citizens run from their burning homes. Wherever you look there is evidence of the X-wings' destructive power.

"Is our ship in good enough shape to take on the remaining X-wings?" Q-7N asks.

"Let's hope so," you reply. You pull the Y-wing upward until you have a wide view of the city. In the distance, three X-wings are concentrating their attack on a tall tower. Immense metal spikes angle outward from its peak.

"That tower doesn't look like the other buildings," Q-7N observes.

"That's because it's a power station," you inform the droid. "If the Imperials blow it up, the blast would wipe out the whole mountain!" You angle the Y-wing and begin your approach to the tower.

"Why are you so determined to prevent the Empire from destroying their own station?" Q-7N asks. "It seems to me they're just doing the job for the Rebels."

"The Rebel Alliance fights its own battles, Q-7N," you answer. "I won't have anyone thinking that Rebels are responsible for a cowardly attack on Delrakkin. Also, the Empire must be doing this for a reason — a reason which can't be good for the Rebellion."

The Y-wing dives toward a single X-wing as you trigger your laser cannons.

To combat the X-wing: Add your skill# and your Y-wing's weaponry# +3 to your stealth# for your confront#. Roll the 12-dice to blow the wings off of the Imperial pilot's ship.

If your confront# is equal to or more than your roll#, add the difference to your MP total. The fractured X-wing plummets to the streets below in a fiery spectacle. You can now proceed.

If your confront# is less than your roll#, subtract the difference from your MP total and repeat this confront using the same confront# until you have destroyed the X-wing. After the X-wing goes down in flames, you may proceed.

The exploding X-wing gains the attention of the two other Imperial pilots. They cease fire on the power station and fly toward your Y-wing.

You may either combat both X-wings at once, or one at a time.

To combat both X-wings at once: Add your Y-wing's weaponry# to your skill# +3 for your confront#. Roll the 12-dice to shoot a giant metal spike off the power station.

If your confront# is equal to or more than your roll#, add 7MP to your MP total. The long metal spike topples down on the two X-wings and sends them crashing into the base of the station. You may now proceed.

If your confront# is lower than your roll#, subtract the difference from your MP total. Now add +3 to your confront# for your new confront#. Roll the 12-dice again to fire another blast at the metal spike.

If your new confront# is equal to or more than your roll#, add the difference to your MP total, then proceed.

If your new confront# is less than your roll#, subtract the difference from your MP total. Repeat this confront with your new confront# until you have defeated the two X-wings, then proceed.

To combat one X-wing at a time: Add your Y-wing's weaponry# to your skill# +1 for your confront#. Roll the 6-dice to fire at the first X-wing.

If your confront# is equal to or more than your roll#, add 5MP to your MP total. You may proceed to the second X-wing, using the same confront equation.

If your confront# is less than your roll#, subtract the difference from your MP total and repeat this confront, adding +1 to your confront# for your new confront#. Once you have defeated the first X-wing, repeat this confront for the second X-wing, using your first confront#. After you have defeated the second X-wing, you may proceed.

You've prevented the X-wings from destroying the power station — add 20MP to your MP total (35 MP for Advanced Level players).

"Where are the other X-wings?" Q-7N wonders aloud. "There are still twelve left, you know."

"I can count, Q-7N," you reply. "Maybe the two squadrons were assigned to different parts of the city. We'll take a wide pass overhead and locate them."

"Is that a good idea?" asks the droid.

"Probably not," you reply, "but it's the only one I have!"

The Y-wing rises high above the mountaintop, and you spot the X-wings at the far side of Delrakkin City. Smoke billows up from a number of tall buildings.

You speed to the scene and target an X-wing that has broken away from the others. "This is too easy," you mutter.

Just before you fire, the X-wing accelerates and whips sharply around a skyscraper.

"He knows I'm on to him!" you shout. "He'll be waiting for me around that corner!"

You dive and wrap around the skyscraper, rising from a point lower than the X-wing's path. The X-wing turns and fires, but your approach is below the Imperial pilot's calculation. The laser blasts pass over your ship as you lock on your target. You fire — and hit!

You rise away from the skyscraper and loop back toward the other X-wings. But when you swing low over a row of flaming buildings, the X-wings are gone.

"Where did they all —" Q-7N begins, but his words are interrupted by a hail of laser blasts as eleven X-wings rise from alleys between the buildings, firing at your ship.

"It's a trap!" you yell as one blast hits your left sensor array and the Y-wing goes into a spin. You pull hard on the controls and accelerate. Smoke trails off your left wing.

There are too many X-wings aiming their laser cannons at you. You must either hide from them or outrun them.

To outrun the X-wings: Your skill# + your vehicle's speed# is your confront#. Roll the 6-dice to speed your way out of this one.

If your confront# is equal to or more than your roll#, add the difference to your MP total. You've tapped your sublight engine and have blasted away before the Imperial pilots could catch you.

If your confront# is less than your roll#, subtract the difference from your MP total. You must try again. Use the same confront# to repeat this confront until you have gotten away.

To hide from the X-wings (without Power): Your Y-wing's stealth# + your stealth# +3 is your confront#. Roll the 12-dice to evade the X-wings.

If your confront# is equal to or more than your roll#, add the difference to your MP total. You've found a hiding place in the peaks of Delrakkin City and have lost the Imperial pilots before they could fire.

If your confront# is less than your roll#, subtract the difference from your MP total and repeat this confront, adding +2 to your confront# for your new confront#.

To hide from the X-wings (using Power)*: Choose your Vehicle Evasion Power. Add your Jedi# and your stealth# to your Y-wing's stealth# and your Power's mid-resist# for your confront#. Roll the 6-dice to evade the Imperial pilots.

If your confront# is equal to or more than your roll#, add the difference to your MP total. Instead of your Y-wing, the Imperial pilots think they see a TIE Advanced x1 prototype and hold their fire while you make your escape. You can now proceed.

If your confront# is lower than your roll#, subtract the difference from your MP total and repeat this confront.

*Note: This counts as one of two Power uses you are allowed in this Mission.

"I can't believe I fell for that!" you admit. "The first X-wing distracted me, but he was just a sacrifice to set me up for the other ships!"

"You'd better fly faster!" Q-7N cries as it looks out the rear window. "You may have escaped that gauntlet, but the X-wings are coming after you again."

"We'll never make it back into space with all of them after me," you respond. "I'll have to try making it back to the jungle."

Dodging laser blasts from behind, the Y-wing tears down the streets and soars to the edge of the city. You take the Y-wing into a sharp dive over the side of the mountain. The Y-wing's hull nearly scrapes the rocky mountain wall as you plunge faster through the clouds toward the jungle below.

An X-wing shoots and hits your right exhaust nacette. Your shields absorb most of the impact, but you have to struggle to keep control of your ship. The foothills of the mountain come into sight, and you angle your ship in a dangerous arc, followed by eleven screaming X-wings.

Another blast from behind hits the Y-wing and you dip dangerously close to the ground.

"There's too much damage!" you shout as you swoop over the foothills. "Get up front, Q-7N. We have to eject!"

Q-7N bounces off the canopy ceiling in a hasty jump to the front seat. You tuck the droid inside your vest and push the ejector button.

The canopy flies open and your seat blasts out of the Y-wing. Luckily, this Y-wing is specially equipped with a paraglider. You soar into the sky and your chute releases it. Glancing in the direction of your Y-wing, you watch as it crashes and cartwheels into an explosive roll of flame.

"What happened?" asks Q-7N as you glide above the trees. You open your vest and release the small droid into the air. As Q-7N looks toward the burning Y-wing, you both hear the oncoming X-wings.

"They're heading right for us!" Q-7N yelps. "Can't you reach the ground any faster?!"

"Yes, I can," you reply as you grab Q-7N and stuff the droid back into your vest. "But it's going to be a rough landing!" You reach for your scimitar or lightsaber.

To cut the harness: Your skill# + your weapon's close-range# is your confront#. Roll the 6-dice to cut the harness to your paraglider so you can fall to the trees below.

> If your confront# is equal to or more than your roll#, add the difference to your MP total. You have landed safely in the trees and can proceed.

> If your confront# is lower than your roll#, subtract the difference from your MP total. You must try again! Repeat this confront until you have landed in the trees, then proceed.

You drop from the trees and open your vest. Q-7N flies out and turns all three photoreceptors to you. "Why did you drag me down with you?!" demands the droid. "I could have floated to the ground!"

"I guess I enjoy your company too much," you reply with a smirk.

Overhead, the Imperial pilots break their formation. Eight of the X-wings soar high into the sky. The other three X-wings circle back toward your position.

"Where are the eight ships going?" asks Q-7N.

"Probably back to where they came from, but it's the remaining three that worry me."

The three X-wings swoop down, spewing a path of laser fire at you. Running as fast as you can, you chase after Q-7N and leap behind an outcropping of rocks.

Q-7N steals a glance over the rocks. "The X-wings are landing!" warns the droid. Seconds later, the droid adds, "The pilots have climbed out of their ships and are walking this way!"

"Great!" you mutter as you draw your weapon. "Only three against one!"

"One? What about me?"

"Sorry, but you're not equipped with a blaster!"

"Surrender, Rebel scum!" exclaims an Imperial pilot as he leaps into view.

You must combat the Imperial pilot.

To combat the Imperial pilot: Choose your weapon. Your weaponry# + weapon's mid-range# is your confront#. Roll the 6-dice to blow the pilot out of his Imperial boots.

If your confront# is equal to or more than your roll#, add the difference to your MP total and proceed.

If your confront# is lower than your roll#, subtract the difference from your MP total. Now double your confront# and add +1 for your new confront#. Roll the

12-dice to fire another blast at the stubborn Imperial pilot.

If your new confront# is equal to or more than your roll#, you may proceed.

If your new confront# is less than your roll#, subtract the difference from your MP total. Add +1 to your confront#. Repeat this confront with your new confront# until you have defeated the Imperial pilot, then proceed.

Q-7N spies a dark crevice among the rocks. "Look over there — I think it's an entrance to a cave!"

"We might stand a better chance of survival in there," you consider, following the floating droid into the cave.

"Careful," cautions Q-7N. "It's pretty dark in here."

"I can't see anything!" you whisper in response.

Q-7N is suddenly illuminated by several small white lights. "This will certainly run down my battery, but now you can see where we're going. I'll use my infrared lens for myself and lead the way."

You move deeper into the cave until you reach a large chamber. Somewhere in the distance, you hear water dripping.

Something big shifts in the shadows. A deep, mysterious voice asks, "Who goes there?"

"I'm a pilot," you reply. "My ship crashed. I'm being pursued by a dangerous enemy."

Light fills the chamber as a dozen torches burst into flame. Q-7N flies protectively in front of you.

Eight native Delrakkins surround you. They are lizard-like in appearance and their hairless skin is pale green. All of them carry picks and shovels. The creature standing closest to you is a tall female.

"Who is your enemy?" asks the deep-voiced creature. She appears to be the leader.

Q-7N flies beside your head and whispers in your ear. "I think you should tell the truth."

"I'm with the Rebel Alliance," you confess. "My enemy is the Empire!"

"Your enemy is ours," replies the creature. "My name is Untrilla. We shall aid you."

"Wait!" cries another native. He is a broad-shouldered creature with hatred in his yellow eyes. "The humans have always lied to us. Let this one take the test to gain our trust!"

"Test?" you ask. "What kind of test?"

The other creatures nod in agreement and begin to chant. Your challenger drops his digging tools to the ground. "You and I must fight!"

Glancing at Q-7N, you mutter, "This is what I get for telling the truth?"

You can choose to fight the native or talk your way out of a fight. You must choose now, then proceed.

To talk your way out of the fight (without Power): Your charm# +1 is your confront#. Roll the 6-dice to peacefully convey your sincerity to the creatures.

If your confront# is equal to or more than your roll#, add the difference to your MP total. The Delrakkins are moved by your profound ability to communicate.

If your confront# is lower than your roll#, subtract the difference from your MP total. The natives think you're as trustworthy as a Hutt and now you'll have to fight (below).

To talk your way out of the fight (using Power)*: Choose your Persuasion Power. Your charm# + your Power's mid-resist# + your Jedi# is your confront#. Roll the 6-dice to convince the Delrakkins that you are telling the truth.

If your confront# is equal to or more than your roll#, add the difference to your MP total. You have convinced the Delrakkins that you come in peace. You may now proceed.

If your confront# is less than your roll#, subtract the difference from your MP total. Your Persuasion has failed. You must fight (below).

*Note: This counts as one of two Power uses you are allowed in this Mission.

To combat the native Delrakkin: Add your strength# to your skill# for your confront#. Roll the 6-dice to throw a punch at your opponent.

If your confront# is equal to or more than your roll#, add the difference to your MP total. Your powerful punch barely affected your opponent, but he knows you are willing to fight for your beliefs. You have earned his respect and may proceed.

If your confront# is lower than your roll#, subtract the difference from your MP total. Now add +1 to your confront# for your new confront#. Roll the 6-dice again to lob another blow at the creature.

> *If your new confront# is equal to or more than your roll#,* you may proceed.

> *If your new confront# is less than your roll#,* subtract the difference from your MP total. Repeat this confront with your new confront# until you have landed a punch on the creature, then proceed.

You have gained a new ally. Add 15MP to your MP total (25 MP for Advanced Level players) and proceed.

"Congratulations," Untrilla says. "You handled yourself very well."

"And you have gained my respect," adds the muscular challenger. "My name is Gwann, and we are at your service."

"For what it's worth, I don't enjoy fighting," you declare. "But if there's one thing worth fighting, it's Imperial tyranny!"

"We agree," Untrilla responds. "Tell us, why have you come to Delrakkin?"

"My friends and I were attacked by Imperials disguised as Rebel pilots. We had to land our freighter, and I pursued the Imperials. The Empire has instigated a complicated plan involving contaminated bacta. I don't know much more than that. But you may be in danger. All I know is it involves bacta."

Hearing the word *bacta*, Untrilla and Gwann exchange glances. Untrilla looks in your direction, narrows her eyes, and orders you to explain further.

"We believe a shipment of contaminated bacta was being transported to Delrakkin," you begin, "but the shipment was destroyed. We know a Carrack cruiser brought alazhi from Thyferra to the Delrakkin system, and we suspect the Empire may have planted the alazhi on your planet."

Gwann's face is suddenly transformed to a darker shade of green. "A Carrack cruiser visited here a few weeks ago," Gwann states. "But it was not an Imperial ship."

"What do you mean?" you ask, surprised. "Wasn't it carrying three TIE fighters?"

"No," Gwann replies. "It carried three X-wings. The Carrack's pilot told us he was a Rebel. He said he had captured the cruiser from the Empire, and it was now part of the Rebel fleet. We saw the X-wings and believed him."

"He asked us to help him plant alazhi," adds Untrilla. "He said the Rebels hoped to produce bacta on Delrakkin so they would not have to rely on Thyferran sources. We do not believe alazhi will grow here, but we are willing to help the Rebellion."

"Did the Carrack's pilot give you his name?" you ask.

"Yes," Untrilla replies. "He said his name was Skeezer."

You feel your anger build as you repeat the name. "Skeezer! I assure you, this man is *not* with the Alliance! He's a captain with the Imperial Navy! We recently captured him and his cruiser."

"But what about the X-wings he'd had?" Gwann asks.

"The Empire got ahold of at least twenty-four X-wings,"

you reply. "I'm telling you, this is all part of some elaborate plot —"

"Nobody move!" a voice commands from the back of the cave. You recognize the metallic voice of an Imperial pilot and realize he has succeeded in tracking you down. "You are all under arrest!"

You don't want any innocent Delrakkins to get shot. "Everyone drop to the floor!" you yell. As the natives fall to the ground, you pivot and draw your weapon.

To combat the Imperial pilot: Choose your weapon. Add your weaponry# to your weapon's mid-range# for your confront#. Roll the 6-dice to shoot the Imperial pilot.

If your confront# is equal to or more than your roll#, add the difference to your MP total and proceed.

If your confront# is lower than your roll#, subtract the difference from your MP total. Repeat the confront until you have neutralized the Imperial pilot, then proceed.

"That was some shooting!" Q-7N exclaims.

"Thanks," you reply. "I have an idea about how to get more answers. First, I have to get this pilot out of his suit."

The Delrakkins assist you. In minutes, you are wearing the black-armored uniform of the Imperial starpilot. "I hate these helmets," you admit as you place it over your head, "but it may be the best way to get close to the enemy!"

"What will you do now?" asks Untrilla.

"There's another Imperial pilot out there," you answer. "I'm going to try to find out the details of this mission."

"Is there anything we can do to help?" asks Gwann.

"Yes. My friends are probably still trying to repair our freighter, the *Millennium Falcon*. If you can reach them, you could tell them I might be leaving Delrakkin, but I'll try to return with help as soon as possible."

Q-7N gives the precise location of the *Falcon* to the Delrakkins.

"We will tell your friends," promises Untrilla. "Thank you for trying to help us."

"Until you hear from the Rebellion," you warn, "beware of anyone trying to give you any bacta!"

With Q-7N hovering at your side, you turn and make your way out of the cave. Although the Imperial helmet is uncomfortable, the infrared lenses allow you to see in the dark. As you approach the exit of the cave, you tuck Q-7N into a flight suit pocket where the droid won't be seen.

The surviving Imperial pilot stands waiting outside the cave next to the body of the first fallen pilot. "Did you find the Rebel?" asks the black-suited figure.

"Yes," you reply. "I shot him."

"Admiral Termo will be disappointed," mutters the pilot. "While you were in the cave, I received a transmission from the *Liquidator*. Termo wanted the Y-wing pilot captured alive!"

"It's too late for that," you respond. Your brain is on overdrive. You remember the name *Liquidator* as an Imperial-class Star Destroyer. "We'd better get back to the ship."

You walk with the Imperial pilot in silence back to the three X-wings. "What'll we do about the third ship?" you ask the pilot.

"Leave it," replies the pilot as he walks to his X-wing. "We'll send a team down to recover it."

You walk to one of the two other X-wings and climb up to the cockpit.

"Hey!" calls the pilot from the seat of his X-wing. "Why are you getting into 2249's ship?"

You realize 2249 must have been the pilot you shot outside the cave. "I'm just making sure the canopy is locked," you reply, thinking fast. "I don't want any of those filthy natives crawling around in our X-wings."

"Good thinking," comments the pilot as he pulls down his own canopy.

As you walk to the other X-wing, Q-7N trembles slightly in its hiding place. "That was good thinking," whispers the droid. "I was wondering how you would explain climbing into the wrong ship!"

You climb into the X-wing and fire up the engines. Activating your comm unit, you address the Imperial pilot. "My nav computer appears to be damaged," you announce. "Can you fly lead back to the *Liquidator*?"

"Stay on my starboard wing," responds the pilot.

The two X-wings blast away from Delrakkin. In minutes, you are in space, sticking close to the Imperial pilot's ship. Q-7N remains silent as you fly toward a nearby moon.

On the far side of the moon, you see a giant dark wedge against the stars. Except for its running lights, the *Liquidator* is almost invisible in the shadow of the moon. You follow the X-wing into the primary docking bay but remain in your ship as the other lands.

The nine X-wings are lined up in a neat row. Beyond the X-wings you see a large fuel storage tank. One direct hit to the tank should take out most of the X-wings.

"Oh, well," you tell Q-7N. "Here goes nothing!"

To shoot the fuel storage tank: Add your skill# to your X-wing's weaponry# +1 for your confront#. Roll the 6-dice to fire a blast at the fuel storage tank.

> *If your confront# is equal to or more than your roll#,* add the difference to your MP total. The fuel storage tank erupts in a massive explosion that shatters the landed X-wings. You can now proceed.

> *If your confront# is less than your roll#,* subtract the difference from your MP total. Repeat this confront until you have shot the storage tank, then proceed.

The power of the explosion knocks your ship to the far side of the hangar. You throw open the canopy and leap out of the X-wing. Your ship is a bit singed, but it is not damaged.

"You there!" yells the Imperial pilot who led you to the *Liquidator*. He is backed by another pilot. "You fired that blast deliberately!"

You can choose to talk your way out or fight the two pilots. If you choose to fight, you can combat them both at once or one at a time.

To talk your way out (without Power): Your charm# +1 is your confront#. Roll the 6-dice to tell the Imperial pilots that your weapons system malfunctioned and you're very, very sorry.

If your confront# is equal to or more than your roll#, add the difference to your MP total. The stupid Imperial pilots fell for your ridiculous excuse. You may now proceed.

If your confront# is less than your roll#, subtract the difference from your MP total. The Imperial pilots think your excuse is incredibly lame and draw their weapons. You must proceed to combat the pilots. Choose now whether to combat both pilots at once or one at a time, then proceed (below).

To talk your way out (using Power)*: Choose your Persuasion Power. Your charm# + your Power's mid-resist# + your Jedi# is your confront#. Roll the 6-dice to tell the Imperial pilots that your weapons system malfunctioned and you're very, very sorry.

If your confront# is equal to or more than your roll#, add the difference to your MP total. You have powerfully persuaded the pilots that your weapon malfunctioned. You may now proceed.

If your confront# is less than your roll#, subtract the difference from your MP total. The pilots don't believe your story for a second. They draw their weapons. You must fight them. Choose now whether to combat both pilots at once or one at a time, then proceed (below).

*Note: This counts as one of two Power uses you are allowed in this Mission.

To combat both Imperial pilots at once: Choose your weapon. Add your weaponry# to your weapon's far-range# for your confront#. Roll the 6-dice to blast a cable that secures a stack of waste barrels.

If your confront# is equal to or more than your roll#, add the difference to your MP total. The barrels tumble down upon the two pilots and knock them flat. You may now proceed.

If your confront# is lower than your roll#, subtract the difference from your MP total. Now add +1 to your confront# for your new confront#. Roll the 6-dice again to fire again at the cable.

If your new confront# is equal to or more than your roll#, add the difference to your MP total, then proceed.

If your new confront# is less than your roll#, subtract the difference from your MP total. The pilots have advanced and you must combat them one at a time (below).

To combat one Imperial pilot at a time: Choose your weapon. Your weaponry# + your weapon's mid-range# is your confront#. Roll the 6-dice to shoot the first Imperial pilot.

If your confront# is equal to or more than your roll#, add the difference to your MP total. You may proceed to the second Imperial pilot, using the same confront equation.

If your confront# is less than your roll#, subtract the difference from your MP total and repeat this confront, adding +4 to your confront# for your new confront#.

Using your new confront#, roll the 12-dice to shoot the pilot. Repeat this confront with the same new confront# to combat the second pilot. Once you have defeated both Imperial pilots, you may proceed.

For your great progress, add 25MP to your MP total (40 MP for Advanced Level players).

You run for a hydrolift. Once inside, you release Q-7N from the pocket of your flight suit. As you rise to an upper level, a voice speaks over the elevator's comm unit.

"Bridge to landing bay!" calls the voice. "The computer reports a massive explosion in the hangar. Explain your situation!"

"Number 2249 to the bridge!" you yell into the comm unit. "Rebel spies have penetrated the landing bay! There are hundreds of them, and they're disguised as stormtroopers!" You unholster your blaster.

"We receive, 2249!" answers the voice over the comm. "Maintain your present position until —"

The voice is interrupted by your blaster as you fire into the comm unit.

"Why did you do that?!" asks Q-7N.

"To keep them wondering," you reply. "With any luck, the stormtroopers will start shooting at each other!"

The elevator doors slide open and you step into a corridor. Imperial officers run past you. Trying your best to blend into the crowd, you press forward.

"Which way now?" Q-7N inquires.

"I'm not sure," you answer as you sidestep an apparently anxious mouse droid. "We need to find out about the bacta, but I don't know where to begin."

"What about the ship's computers?" Q-7N suggests.

"I'd need an R2 unit for that," you reply.

"Sorry I'm not an astromech," Q-7N apologizes.

A stormtrooper sentry blocks your path. "Halt!" he orders. "Why are you on the officers' quarters level?"

You can either lie to the stormtrooper, run away from him, punch him, or use a weapon against him.

To lie to the stormtrooper (without Power): Your charm# is your confront#. Roll the 6-dice to tell the stormtrooper that you happen to be an Imperial officer, and if he doesn't get out of your way, you will put him on report.

> *If your confront# is equal to or more than your roll#,* add the difference to your MP total. The stormtrooper steps aside and you can proceed.

> *If your confront# is less than your roll#,* subtract the difference from your MP total. The stormtrooper knows you're bluffing and reaches for his weapon. You'll have to either punch him or use your weapon against him (below).

To lie to the stormtrooper (using Power)*: Choose your Persuasion Power. Your charm# + your Power's mid-resist# + your Jedi# is your confront#. Roll the 6-dice to convince the stormtrooper that you are an Imperial officer, who will get him into trouble if he does not let you pass.

> *If your confront# is equal to or more than your roll#,* add the difference to your MP total. The stormtrooper believes you are an officer. You may now proceed.

If your confront# is less than your roll#, subtract the difference from your MP total. The stormtrooper realizes what you really are — a Rebel! You must combat him. Choose either to punch him or to use your weapon (below).

*Note: This counts as one of two Power uses you are allowed in this Mission.

To run away from the stormtrooper: Your skill# + 1 is your confront#. Roll the 6-dice to escape.

If your confront# is equal to or more than your roll#, add the difference to your MP total. You've left the stormtrooper in the dust. You may now proceed.

If your confront# is less than your roll#, subtract the difference from your MP total. Your escape attempt has failed. You must combat him. Choose either to punch him or to use your weapon (below).

To use a weapon to combat the stormtrooper: Choose your weapon. Your weaponry# + your weapon's close-range# is your confront#. Roll the 6-dice to fight.

If your confront# is equal to or more than your roll#, add the difference to your MP total. The stormtrooper is now out of commission. You may proceed.

If your confront# is less than your roll#, subtract the difference from your MP total. You must try again. Use the same confront# and repeat this confront until you have neutralized the stormtrooper.

To punch the stormtrooper: Your strength# +1 is your confront#. Roll the 6-dice to throw a left hook that will make the stormtrooper wish he'd never seen you.

If your confront# is equal to or more than your roll#, add the difference to your MP total. The stormtrooper is lifted off the floor by the power of your punch and he lands with a satisfying thud. You may now proceed.

If your confront# is lower than your roll#, subtract the difference from your MP total. Now double your confront# for your new confront#. Roll the 12-dice to throw another punch at the antagonistic stormtrooper.

If your new confront# is equal to or more than your roll#, add the difference to your MP total, then proceed.

If your new confront# is less than your roll#, subtract the difference from your MP total. Repeat this confront with your new confront# until you have vanquished the stormtrooper, then proceed.

You move hastily away from the stormtrooper.

"Don't leave without me!" Q-7N cries as it flies to catch up with you.

"I've studied the layouts of Star Destroyers," you tell him. "If I remember correctly, the Admiral's quarters should be at the end of this corridor!"

"What will we find there?"

"A clue, I hope. Maybe we'll even run into the Admiral himself!"

The door at the end of the hallway is locked but unguarded.

"How will we get in?" asks the floating droid.

"Watch," you answer as you raise your weapon.

You can either try to hotwire the lock or shoot open the door.

To hotwire the lock: Your skill# +2 is your confront#. Roll the 6-dice to try to open the lock.

> If your confront# is equal to or more than your roll#, add the difference to your MP total. The lock is open. You push open the door and proceed.

> If your confront# is less than your roll#, subtract the difference from your MP total. You must try again. Use the same confront# and repeat this confront until you have opened the lock.

To shoot open the door: Choose your weapon. Your weaponry# + your weapon's close-range# is your confront#. Roll the 6-dice to blast the security lock at the side of the door.

> If your confront# is equal to or more than your roll#, add the difference to your MP total. The door slides open and you proceed.

> If your confront# is less than your roll#, subtract the difference from your MP total. Repeat this confront until you have blasted the lock and opened the door.

Admiral Termo's private quarters are empty. A holoprojector sits on the desk.

"It doesn't look like there's much to find here," you confess as you search the room.

"This is interesting," Q-7N comments. "My sensors indicate this desktop is actually a safe."

Your fingers glide over the surface of the desktop. "I should be able to manage this," you proclaim.

To open the safe (without Power): Your skill# +2 is your confront#. Roll the 6-dice to open the desk safe.

If your confront# is equal to or more than your roll#, add the difference to your MP total. The desktop slides away to reveal the contents of the safe. You can now proceed.

If your confront# is less than your roll#, subtract the difference from your MP total. Repeat this confront until you have opened the safe, then proceed.

To open the safe (using Power)*: Choose your Object Movement Power. Your skill# + your Power's mid-resist# + your Jedi# is your confront#. Roll the 6-dice to open the safe.

If your confront# is equal to or more than your roll#, add the difference to your MP total. The desktop slides away to reveal the contents of the safe. You may proceed.

If your confront# is less than your roll#, subtract the difference from your MP total. Repeat this confront until you have opened the safe, then proceed.

*Note: this counts as one of two Power uses you are allowed in this Mission.

As soon as you open the safe, a loud alarm sounds. The safe contains two holotapes. You grab the holotapes and shove them into your flightsuit pocket. "Come on, Q-7N!" you yell as you run for the door. "Let's get out of here!"

Q-7N flies beside you as you run back to the hydrolift. "We're going back to the hangar, aren't we?" the droid asks as you press a button to descend.

"Why not?" you reply, tapping the breastplate of your flight suit armor. "I'm dressed for it!"

The hydrolift reaches the hangar and you run for your X-wing. Rescue and repair crews are all over the place, trying to extinguish fires. You jump into your X-wing with Q-7N.

Gunning the engines, you steer the X-wing out of the hangar and blast away from the Star Destroyer. Suddenly, the X-wing jolts to a stop and its engines whine under immense pressure.

"They've locked us into their tractor beam!" you exclaim. Putting the ship into a spin, you aim the X-wing's guns at the tractor beam projector.

To knock out the tractor beam projector: Choose your weapon. Add your weaponry# + skill# to the X-wing's weaponry# +2 for your confront#. Roll the 12-dice to shoot the tractor beam projector.

If your confront# is equal to or more than your roll#, add the difference to your MP total. The tractor beam projector erupts in a ball of fire and you can proceed.

If your confront# is less than your roll#, subtract the difference from your MP total. Repeat this confront until you have destroyed the tractor beam projector, then proceed.

Tearing away from the *Liquidator*, you cast a glance behind you in time to see six TIE fighters launch out of the secondary launch bay. You speed toward Delrakkin's airless moon.

The TIE fighters split into two attack formations. You steer the X-wing down toward the surface of the moon. You're so close you can see the X-wing's shadow glide across the rocky terrain.

Laser fire rips past your ship and you push the X-wing hard to the side, swooping down into a gray ravine. A natural bridge looms ahead and you fly lower until you pass under the formation.

"A direct hit to that bridge could bring down the three TIE fighters that are right behind us!" you say aloud.

"That's a difficult shot," comments Q-7N. "It might be better if you tried attacking the ships directly!"

You pull the X-wing into a loop and aim.

Choose to fight the TIE fighters all at once (by shooting the bridge) or one at a time.

To destroy the three TIE fighters at once: Choose your weapon. Add your weaponry# + your skill# to the X-wing's weaponry# for your confront#. Roll the 12-dice to fire at the bridge.

If your confront# is equal to or more than your roll#, add 9MP to your MP total. The bridge comes crashing down on top of the three TIE fighters. You may proceed.

If your confront# is lower than your roll#, subtract the difference from your MP total. Now add +4 to your confront# for your new confront#. Roll the 12-dice again to fire another blast at the natural bridge.

If your new confront# is equal to or more than your roll#, add the difference to your MP total, then proceed.

If your new confront# is less than your roll#, subtract the difference from your MP total. You have missed your opportunity to blast the natural bridge and you must combat the TIE fighters one at a time (below).

To destroy one TIE fighter at a time: Choose your weapon. Your weaponry# + your X-wing's weaponry# +3 is your confront#. Roll the 12-dice to combat the first TIE fighter.

If your confront# is equal to or more than your roll#, add the difference to your MP total. Proceed to combat the second TIE fighter, using the same confront equation.

If your confront# is less than your roll#, subtract the difference from your MP total and repeat this confront, adding +2 to your confront# for your new confront#. Once you have defeated the first TIE fighter, repeat this confront (without changing the confront#) for the second and third TIE fighters. Once you have defeated all three TIE fighters, you may proceed.

* * *

You're barely away from the bridge when the second group of TIE fighters begins its attack. Blaster fire strikes your rear deflector shields as you lift the X-wing up into space. You knife sharply downwards, aiming for a large cavernous hole.

"You're not going into that crater?!" Q-7N yelps, terrified.

"They'd be crazy to follow me in there!" you answer, trying to stay calm.

The TIE fighters pursue you into the crater, illuminating the darkness with the blasts from their laser cannons.

A warning light flashes on the X-wing's dashboard. "Don't tell me you're going to hit a dead end!" cries Q-7N.

"Okay, I won't tell you!" you reply as you hit the inertial dampers. Thrown into a tight spin, the X-wing reverses its angle and you come up facing the oncoming TIE fighters.

Choose to combat or evade the oncoming TIE fighters. If you choose to combat, know that you are choosing to combat all of the TIE fighters at once. If you choose to evade, you can choose to evade with Power or without. You must choose now, before you proceed.

To evade the TIE fighters (without Power): Your skill + your X-wing's stealth# is your confront#. Roll the 6-dice to dodge the TIE fighters and fly out of the crater.

If your confront# is equal to or more than your roll#, add the difference to your MP total. You pass the TIE fighters and the three ships crash into the bottom of the crater. You can proceed.

If your confront# is lower than your roll#, subtract the difference from your MP total. You've missed your chance to escape and now you must combat the TIE fighters (below).

To evade the TIE fighters (using Power)*: Choose your Vehicle Evasion Power. Your Jedi# + your Power's mid-resist# + your X-wing's stealth# is your confront#. Roll the 6-dice to evade the Imperial pilots.

If your confront# is equal to or more than your roll#, add the difference to your MP total. The Imperial pilots miscalculate their distances. Confused, they panic and smash into the walls of the crater.

If your confront# is lower than your roll#, subtract the difference from your MP total and repeat this confront until you have evaded the TIE fighters.

*Note: This counts as one of two Power uses you are allowed in this Mission.

To combat the TIE fighters: Add your weaponry# + your X-wing's weaponry# to your skill# +2 for your confront#. Roll the 12-dice to blast the central TIE fighter.

If your confront# is equal to or more than your roll#, add the difference to your MP total. The central TIE fighter explodes and its pieces fly outward into the paths of the two other ships, causing them to crash.

If your confront# is lower than your roll#, subtract the difference from your MP total. Now add +3 to your confront# for your new confront#. Roll the 12-dice again to continue to fire another blast at the central TIE fighter.

If your new confront# is equal to or more than your roll#, add the difference to your MP total, then proceed.

If your new confront# is less than your roll#, subtract the difference from your MP total. Repeat this confront with your new confront# until you have destroyed the TIE fighters. You may then proceed.

The X-wing launches up and out of the crater.

"Where's the *Liquidator*?" asks Q-7N.

"There's no sign of it on my sensors!" you reply. "It must have gone into hyperspace!"

"Can we follow it?" inquires the droid.

"Not through hyperspace, Q-7N," you answer. "I'll explain the science of hyperspace later. Right now, we've got to go back to Delrakkin and check on the *Falcon*!"

You have performed admirably. Reward yourself 200 MP (275 MP for Advanced Level Players).

THE AFTER-
MISSION

On Delrakkin, Solo and Chewbacca made final repairs to their freighter while Luke and Artoo-Detoo secured the newly acquired X-wing starfighter. Inside the *Millennium Falcon*, Princess Leia, See-Threepio, and Q-7N met with the reptilian natives Untrilla and Gwann in the central hold area.

"Do your people have any idea why the Empire would attack Delrakkin City?" Leia asked the natives.

"We were not allowed into the city, so we can only imagine," Untrilla answered. "But perhaps the Imperial citizens wanted to join the Rebellion. Would that not earn the wrath of the Empire?" •

"We never had any contact from this world," Leia replied. "If the Empire wanted to punish the Imperial citizens, they would have *openly* attacked the city. Instead, they made it look like a Rebel attack. I suspect it has something to do with bacta production."

"If I may say so, Princess Leia," Threepio offered, "perhaps the holotapes from the *Liquidator* might provide some answers?"

Leia nodded. "They just might. We need to deactivate their locking device before we can view them — it should only be a few minutes more. Q-7N, go tell the others to come in here so we can have a look at the holotapes." Q-7N flew out of the chamber.

Soon, everyone was gathered in the *Falcon*'s central hold area.

When the holotapes were ready for viewing, Princess Leia inserted the first one into a slot beneath Artoo-Detoo's domed head. The crew watched in amazement as the ghostly image of Grand Moff Tarkin instructed Termo to contact another Imperial authority. At the end of the message, Artoo ejected the holotape.

"Tarkin ordered Admiral Termo to send 'a coded transmission to destination B90-478R,'" Luke quoted. "Maybe we should send a message and find out who's at the other end of that number."

"And risk revealing our position to the Empire?" Solo scoffed. "Forget it! For all we know, that destination number could be a direct line to the Emperor!"

"Try the second holotape, Artoo," Leia suggested.

The second holotape was activated and Grand Moff Tarkin's image returned.

"Admiral Termo," Tarkin's hologram began, "I hope your conversation with the Emperor went well, but imagine it did not."

Chewbacca eyed Solo and snarled.

"You mean it really *was* the Emperor's number?" muttered an astonished Solo.

"Quiet, Han!" snapped Leia, keeping her eyes on the hologram.

"I'm making this recording," continued Tarkin, "to insure you will carry out your mission on Delrakkin. Although the Empire has spread its power throughout the galaxy, there is a place we have not been able to control. That place is hyperspace itself. For many months, the Empire has been working on a device that will prevent ships from escaping into hyperspace."

"What?!" Solo exclaimed. "That's ridiculous!"

"Shhh!" Leia commanded.

"The Delrakkin system," explained Tarkin's hologram, "is at the end of an old hyperspace trade route. We have chosen Delrakkin as a test site for our experiments and want Delrakkin City for our base of operations. However, our plan is of the utmost secrecy. Despite the fact that Delrakkin City is populated by Imperial citizens, we cannot risk *anyone* discovering our plans. For this reason, the citizens must be *eliminated*."

The effect of Tarkin's words sent chills down the spines of the assembled Rebels.

"The Death Star is transporting a shipment of contaminated bacta," stated Tarkin's hologram. "This bacta carries a virus. It was our intention to deliver the bacta to Delrakkin's medical centers. Within days, all of the citizens would have been dead, and the city would have been ours. The only person on your ship who knew of this plan was Captain Skeezer."

Hearing Skeezer's name, Chewbacca growled. Everyone was glad that he was now in the Rebels' custody on Yavin Four.

"Since the Death Star has not reached its destination," Tarkin's hologram continued, "you must take more dramatic measures. You will tell your troops that Delrakkin City's Imperial citizens intend to join the Rebel Alliance and help the Rebels grow bacta. To support this effort, Captain Skeezer impersonated a Rebel and planted alazhi on Delrakkin. He also acquired twenty-four X-wings for an attack that would be attributed to the Rebel Alliance. If there are any survivors on Delrakkin, they will believe and support our official report that the Rebels were the ones who destroyed their planet."

Grand Moff Tarkin's hologram paused. "Although it sounds unlikely," Tarkin concluded, "it is possible that the

Death Star requires your aid. After you attack Delrakkin, Admiral Termo, you are to travel to the Yavin system and locate the Death Star." The hologram flickered and died.

"Yavin Four!" Leia cried. "The Rebel base!"

"Come on, Chewie," called Solo, racing for the cockpit.

Luke turned to Untrilla and Gwann. "Looks like this is good-bye. Thanks for all your help."

"Good luck," wished Untrilla.

Gwann smiled. "And if you require our help, you know where to find us." The two natives hurried out of the *Falcon* and watched as the Corellian freighter prepared for departure.

"May the Force be with them," whispered Untrilla.

NEXT: DESTROY THE *LIQUIDATOR*